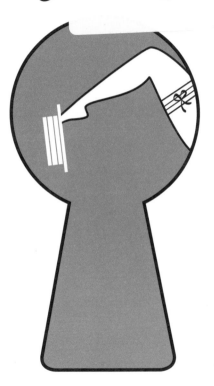

AT iT
AGAiN!

First edition 2012
Second edition 2013
Third edition 2016
Fourth edition 2021

Published by At it Again!
Printed by Plus Print Limited

Text by Niall Laverty and Maite López-Schröder
Illustrations by Niall Laverty

ISBN 978-1-8382229-0-1

www.atitagain.ie

Contents

James Joyce

James Joyce is considered one of the most influential modernist writers of the 20th century. He was born into a Catholic middle-class family in Dublin on the 2 February 1882. But by the time Joyce was a teenager, his father had squandered the family's wealth and they were living on the edge of Monto, Dublin's notorious red-light district.

A cunning linguist, he studied modern languages at University College Dublin (UCD) before going to Paris to study medicine. Instead of learning about dead bodies, he decided to study naked ones, haunting bars and brothels before being called back to Dublin to his dying mother. While back home, he met Galway girl Nora Barnacle, and they eloped to Europe to lead a life of artistic exile, sponging off friends and family until he found patrons to fund his creativity. They lived in Trieste, Zurich and Paris, had two children and secretly married years later in London.

Joyce dabbled in poetry, short stories, plays, novels, singing and selling Irish tweed. He also opened the Volta, Dublin's first cinema. His writing career took off when his collection of short stories, *Dubliners*, was published in 1914 and his novel, *Portrait of the Artist as a Young Man*, two years later. When writing, Joyce liked to have a lazy morning, an industrious afternoon and a chaotic evening. He was a self-declared genius and an outrageous self-publicist. When asked who he thought were the greatest writers in English, Joyce replied, 'Aside from myself? I don't know.'

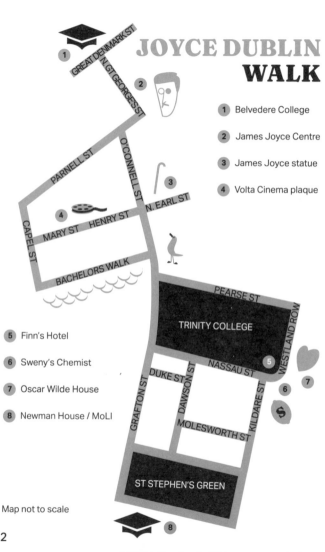

JOYCE DUBLIN WALK

1. Belvedere College
2. James Joyce Centre
3. James Joyce statue
4. Volta Cinema plaque

5. Finn's Hotel
6. Sweny's Chemist
7. Oscar Wilde House
8. Newman House / MoLI

GREAT DENMARK ST
N GT GEORGE'S ST
PARNELL ST
O'CONNELL ST
N. EARL ST
CAPEL ST
MARY ST HENRY ST
BACHELORS WALK
PEARSE ST
TRINITY COLLEGE
WESTLAND ROW
NASSAU ST
GRAFTON ST
DUKE ST
DAWSON ST
KILDARE ST
MOLESWORTH ST
ST STEPHEN'S GREEN

Map not to scale

Ulysses

The story of *Ulysses* is set on 16 June 1904 which has become known as Bloomsday, after the book's protagonist Leopold Bloom and is celebrated every year around the world.

With over 700 pages and no chapter headings, Joyce based his epic tale on Homer's *Odyssey* about a hero's journey home. As the main characters Leopold Bloom and Stephen Dedalus journey across Dublin, they experience all of life in one day. The book is a celebration of the everyday and, like a soap opera, deals with sex, drink, adultery, life and death.

Autobiography and fiction merge, with Joyce basing many of his characters on real people and his native city playing a key role. He joked that Dublin could be rebuilt just from reading *Ulysses*. Joyce takes language on an adventure with his endless wordplay and lets you inside the characters' heads where one thought drifts into the next – known as *stream of consciousness*. You'll discover quirks and contradictions, the weird and the surreal.

Joyce spent seven years composing *Ulysses*. Considered indecent by most publishers, the book was finally published by Sylvia Beach, an American in Paris, in 1922. To critics who found *Ulysses* obscene and unreadable, Joyce said, 'If *Ulysses* isn't fit to read, then life isn't fit to live.'

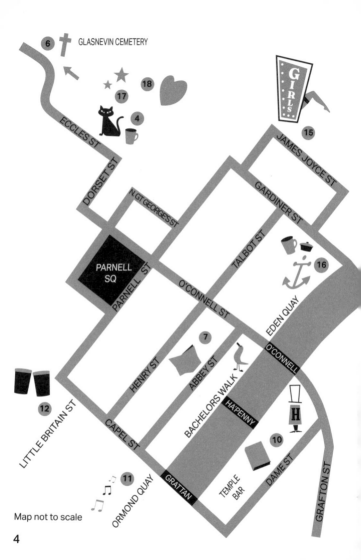

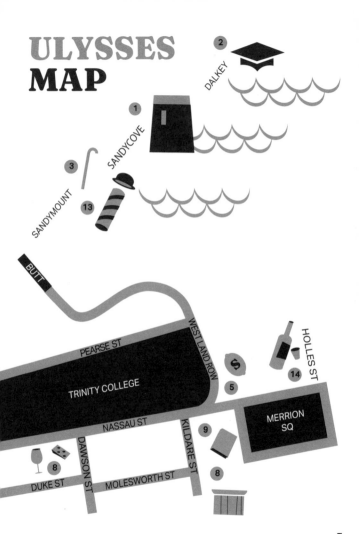

ULYSSES MAP

DALKEY

SANDYCOVE

SANDYMOUNT

13

BUTT

PEARSE ST

WEST LAND ROW

TRINITY COLLEGE

HOLLES ST

5

14

NASSAU ST

MERRION SQ

KILDARE ST

DAWSON ST

9

8

DUKE ST

MOLESWORTH ST

8

How to dress the character

Ulysses is set in the Edwardian era. Here are some ideas for dressing up or check out 'Meet the cast' for more adventurous costumes.

Ladies

In the Edwardian era, royalty and leading actresses inspired fashion. Lighter clothes and colours were all the rage as ladies pursued outdoor sports like tennis, riding and cycling. Curvy figures were created with corsets, padding and petticoats. The two-piece outfit was popular with a tailored jacket and a full-length skirt. Accessories such as a hat and lace gloves were a must.

To create an easy Edwardian look, wear a long skirt with a blouse and jacket. Or pimp an old evening dress. Enhance your curves with a corset or big belt. Decorate a wide straw hat with ribbons, feathers or flowers. To complete the look, add pearls, a cameo brooch or delicate costume jewellery.

Big hair and pale complexions were in. For the pompadour style, backcomb your hair into a big cloud and top it off with a bun. Make-up was subtle, but slap it on if you are feeling naughty.

Gents

King Edward VII was the ultimate trendsetter for the Edwardian gentleman. Most popular was the three-piece suit with a jacket, waistcoat and upturned trousers. Shirts had stiff collars that made turning your head a challenge.

The Edwardian gentleman sported an array of accessories from bow ties and pocket watches to walking sticks with secret compartments. Most importantly, a man of the world wouldn't dream of leaving home without a hat.

To create an easy Edwardian look, pull on a pair of trousers, and a shirt and adorn your neck with a bow tie or handkerchief. Hold up your trousers with a pair of braces and put on a jacket, blazer or waistcoat. Accessorise with spectacles, a walking stick or a flower in your lapel. A hat will finish off your look. Make it a bowler, straw boater or flat cap.

Hair was short and neat, parted down the middle or at the side and slicked back with pomade. Beards were out, and pampered moustaches were in. As a nod to Leopold Bloom, pop a black potato in your pocket for luck before heading out on your epic adventure.

Meet the cast

(In order of appearance)

Malachi 'Buck' Mulligan – Stephen's flamboyant, sharp-tongued flatmate. When he is not swimming in the nude, he wears a yellow dressing gown or his medical-student whites.

Stephen Dedalus – Young teacher and wannabe poet. Back from Paris after the death of his mother, he swans around Dublin with his walking stick getting drunk.

Mr Deasy – Ranting headmaster at Stephen's school who writes angry letters to the press. Shaggy eyebrows and a white moustache lurk beneath his mortar board.

Leopold Bloom – Warm-hearted Jew with an eye for the ladies who is searching for a son. He sweats through the day in a black funeral suit and bowler hat.

Molly Bloom – Concert soprano who enjoys racy novels, breakfast and other activities in bed. Bloom's wife is in and out of her nightie most of the day. Born in Gibraltar, she has a reputation for being hot-blooded.

Blazes Boylan – Man about town, concert tour manager and afternoon lover of Molly Bloom. He flirts his way around Dublin in a straw hat, sky-blue bow tie and a red flower in his buttonhole.

Paddy Dignam – Like many characters in the book, he's ruined by drink. So ruined, it killed him. Ghost-like, he pops up throughout the story.

Hely's Men – Five sandwich-board men advertising a Dublin stationery company. They walk the streets in white smocks and tall white hats bearing red letters that spell out the company name: HELY'S.

Mina Kennedy and **Lydia Douce** – Sirens that tempt gentlemen with song and thigh. One has gold hair, the other bronze. These barmaids keep their customers happy by flashing their garters.

The Citizen – Big bully with an eyepatch who rants about every topic under the sun. He and his scraggly hound Garryowen are regulars in the local boozer.

Gerty MacDowell – Fashionista dressed in blue from head to toe, she even wears blue undies for luck. A young romantic on the beach, she causes a middle-aged man to overheat.

Bella Cohen – Gender-shifting brothel-owner in Dublin's red-light district. She wears an ivory gown and flashes her jewels while brandishing a black fan.

WB Murphy – Shady sailor full of tattoos and tall tales who likes to hang out in late-night joints.

Part 1

MORNING

'Somewhere in the east: early morning: set off at dawn,
travel round in front of the sun, steal a day's march on him.
Keep it up for ever never grow a day older technically.'

Telemachus
The one with the swim

Location 1: The Martello tower in Sandycove

What's the story?

At the Martello tower, Stephen Dedalus, Buck Mulligan and their English tower mate get up. Mulligan goes up to the roof to shave. He imitates a priest celebrating Mass and mocks Stephen for not kneeling down to pray at his mother's deathbed, joking that the shock killed her. They all have breakfast and then head over to the Forty Foot bathing spot where Mulligan dives into the Irish Sea. Splash! Irritated by the others, Stephen leaves for work, vowing never to return.

Why don't you . . . ?

- Visit the James Joyce Tower & Museum in Sandycove.
- Shave, but keep your moustache for the Edwardian look.
- Enjoy a breakfast of eggs, tea, toast, honey and sugar.
- Swim in the Forty Foot or dip your toe into some other watering hole.

He said, she said . . .

'When I makes tea I makes tea, as old mother Grogan said. And when I makes water I makes water.'

BUCK MULLIGAN

Titbit

Traditionally, the Forty Foot was an all-male stronghold for nude bathing. But in the 1970s a female invasion took place that became known as the Attack of the Forty Foot Women.

The snotgreen sea.
The scrotum-tightening sea.

Nestor
The one in school

Location 2: Summerfield House on Dalkey Avenue

What's the story?

Stephen is a disillusioned schoolteacher. He's supposed to be teaching history, but his students are more interested in ghost stories, riddles and hockey. After class, he helps a boy with his sums. It's payday, so Stephen goes to collect his wages from Mr Deasy. The headmaster asks him to use his press contacts to get a letter published. Deasy rants about foot-and-mouth disease, Jews and the state of the nation. Stephen nods and smiles, waiting to be paid.

A coughball of *laughter* leaped from his throat

Why don't you . . . ?

- Explore the seaside village of Dalkey in Co. Dublin.
- Write a letter to a newspaper.
- Have a good old rant.

He said, she said . . .

'History . . . is a nightmare from which I am trying to awake.'
STEPHEN DEDALUS

Titbit

While at school in Belvedere College in Dublin, Joyce was made prefect of the religious society, the Sodality of the Blessed Virgin Mary, and lost his virginity to a prostitute – all in a matter of weeks.

dragging after it a rattling chain of phlegm

Proteus
The one in eternity

Location 3: Sandymount Strand

What's the story?

Taking a stroll on Sandymount Strand, Stephen imagines he's blind and taps along with his cane. He thinks about his dead mother and his writing career. He recalls vivid memories of his recent stay in Paris. Imagination engulfs him, as nearly does the incoming tide. Across the expansive sand a dog bounds. Our bard has a stab at writing a poem and picks his nose.

Why don't you . . . ?

- Walk out into eternity on Sandymount Strand.
- Close your eyes and listen to the sounds around you.
- Write something in the sand.
- Pick your nose.

Do you see the tide flowing quickly in on all sides . . . ?

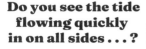

He thought . . .

'Shut your eyes and see.'
STEPHEN DEDALUS

Titbit

Joyce was half-blind towards the end of his life. To be able to read his own work, he had to write in extra-large letters using coloured crayons. Mocking his own literary reputation, he called himself an international eyesore.

Calypso
The one with the shit

Location 4: 7 Eccles Street

What's the story?

Leopold Bloom potters about the kitchen, preparing breakfast and chatting to the cat. He pops out to the butcher's for a kidney where he eyes up the girl next door. Back home, he brings his wife breakfast in bed. Molly tells him that Blazes Boylan is coming for a rendezvous that afternoon. She asks Bloom to pick up a racy novel while he's in town. Armed with a paper, he heads for the outhouse. Splosh!

> **Quietly he read,
> restraining himself,
> the first column and,
> yielding but resisting,
> began the second.**

Why don't you...?

- Visit the James Joyce Centre on North Great George's Street to see the original door of 7 Eccles Street.
- Fry yourself a kidney for breakfast.
- Bring someone breakfast in bed.
- Read the paper on the toilet.

He thought...

'Good puzzle would be cross Dublin without passing a pub.'
LEOPOLD BLOOM

Titbit

The newspaper Bloom is reading on the toilet, is the popular English weekly magazine *Tit-Bits*. It was founded to give the first train commuters a bit of light entertainment on their way to work.

Lotus Eaters
The one with the soap

Location 5: Westland Row and Lincoln Place

What's the story?

At a post office, Bloom collects a letter from Martha, his secret pen pal. A passing acquaintance quizzes him about Molly's upcoming concert tour, alluding to her affair with Blazes Boylan. Bloom pops into St Andrew's Church for some peace and quiet. Floating into Sweny's Chemist, he buys some lemon soap. Back outside, a misunderstanding over a discarded newspaper starts a rumour that Bloom has bet on a 20/1 horse named Throwaway. He ogles women and thinks about taking a Turkish bath.

Why don't you . . . ?

- Visit Sweny's Chemist on Lincoln Place where you can still buy lemon soap.
- Place a bet on a horse with long odds.
- Write a naughty love letter.
- Have a bath.

She wrote . . .

'So now you know what I will do to you, you naughty boy . . .'
MARTHA CLIFFORD

Limp father of thousands, a languid floating flower:

Titbit

Turkish baths were popular in Dublin at the turn of the last century. But they were not just for people. The one on Lincoln Place had a back entrance where horses and other animals could avail of a sauna and massage.

Hades
The one with the funeral

Location 6: Glasnevin Cemetery

What's the story?

Paddy Dignam's funeral procession clip-clops across Dublin from Sandymount to Glasnevin Cemetery. Jostled about in the carriage, Bloom's thoughts meander from life to death. Twelve mourners and a mysterious man in a macintosh pray at the graveside. Bloom thinks about all the decomposing bodies when he spots a fat grey rat.

Why don't you ... ?

- Take a carriage ride.
- Visit Glasnevin Cemetery and find the grave of Joyce's dad, John Stanislaus Joyce.
- Have a drink at the nearby Gravediggers pub where the diggers were served their pints through a hole in the wall.

He thought ...

'As you are now so once were we.'
LEOPOLD BLOOM

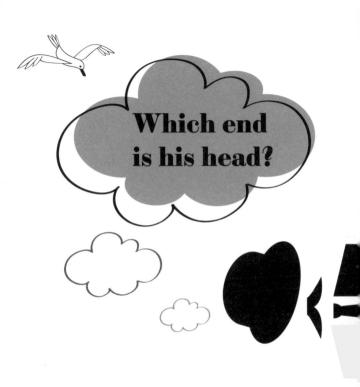

Which end
is his head?

Titbit

Joyce said, 'When I die, Dublin will be written in my heart.' When he died in 1941, the Irish government refused to let him be buried in Ireland, where his books were considered obscene. His body is buried in Fluntern Cemetery in Zurich.

Part 2

AFTERNOON

'The hungry famished gull
Flaps o'er the waters dull.'

Aeolus
The one with the headlines

Location 7: The *Freeman's Journal* on Middle Abbey Street

What's the story?

Bloom goes into the office of the *Freeman's Journal* newspaper to discuss the placement of an advert. There is a lot of hot air talked, and Bloom is blown off course by the rudeness of the editor while the printing presses spit out the daily rag. As he leaves, Stephen comes in to ask for Mr Deasy's letter to be published. The editor agrees, but urges Stephen to write something punchy and original. The newspaper men head over to the Oval Bar for a liquid lunch.

Will you tell him

Why don't you . . . ?

🔹 Pose by the James Joyce statue on North Earl Street.

🔹 Find the former *Irish Independent* newspaper building on Middle Abbey Street and then head over to the nearby Oval Bar for a liquid lunch.

🔹 Visit the National Print Museum on Haddington Road.

He cursed . . .

'Shite and onions!'

STEPHEN DEDALUS'S DAD

Titbit

This episode is full of headlines, and *Ulysses* is the ultimate newspaper capturing life in Dublin on one day. The average newspaper uses 500 different words; *Ulysses* has around 30,000.

he can kiss my arse?

Lestrygonians
The one at lunchtime

Location 8: Middle Abbey Street to the National Museum

What's the story?

After feeding the seagulls by the river Liffey, Bloom goes in search of lunch. On the way, he passes the Hely's men with their tall white hats and bumps into an old flame. Disgusted by the greedy pigs in one restaurant, he ends up in Davy Byrne's pub. While eating gorgonzola cheese and sipping Burgundy wine, he reminisces about making love with Molly on Howth Head. After lunch, he slips into the National Museum to avoid Blazes Boylan. While there, he looks to see if Greek statues have arseholes.

They have no.
Never looked.
I'll look today.
Keeper won't see.

Bend down
let something fall
see if she.

Why don't you . . . ?

- Find the 14 bronze pavement plaques that mark Bloom's lunchtime route.

- Feed the seagulls on O'Connell Bridge.

- Enjoy a gorgonzola sandwich and a glass of Burgundy in Davy Byrne's pub on Duke Street.

He thought . . .

'This is the very worst hour of the day . . . Feel as if I had been eaten and spewed.'

LEOPOLD BLOOM

Titbit

Joyce loved to be the centre of attention at lunches and dinners. On one such occasion, F. Scott Fitzgerald, excited at meeting his idol, offered to jump out of the window in his honour.

Scylla and Charybdis
The one with Shakespeare

2pm

Location 9: The National Library on Kildare Street

What's the story?

Amongst the books in the National Library, Stephen and Buck Mulligan, along with some literary types, hash out theories about Shakespeare's life, inspirations and work. For the sake of an argument, Stephen claims that Shakespeare is Hamlet's father's ghost. Bloom arrives on business of his own, and Mulligan jokes about his sexuality.

Why don't you . . . ?

- Visit the National Library and find the Shakespeare stained-glass window.

- Act out a scene from *Hamlet*.

- Learn more about James Joyce in the Museum of Literature Ireland (MoLI) in Newman House on St Stephen's Green where Joyce once was a student.

- Find the plaque for the original Shakespeare & Co. bookshop, founded by Sylvia Beach, the publisher of *Ulysses*, at 12, rue de l'Odéon in Paris.

He said, she said . . .

'A man of genius makes no mistakes. His errors are volitional and are the portals of discovery.'

STEPHEN DEDALUS

Titbit

During the Nazi occupation of Paris in 1941, Sylvia Beach refused to sell her only copy of Joyce's *Finnegans Wake* to a German officer. He threatened to confiscate all her books. Within a few hours she had removed everything from the shop, painted over the sign and never reopened Shakespeare & Co.

Hamlet, I am thy father's spirit

Wandering Rocks
The one with everyone in it

Location 10: All over Dublin

What's the story?

The Viceroy's carriage crosses the city while a priest surprises young lovers in a hedge. Buck Mulligan scoffs 'damn bad cakes'. Stephen chats in Italian while a crumpled flyer floats down the river Liffey. Bloom hunts for a racy novel for his wife in Merchant's Arch. A coin tossed from Molly's window lands at the foot of a one-legged sailor. Blazes Boylan, ever the scoundrel, flirts with one woman while buying gifts for another.

Why don't you . . . ?

- Give everyone the royal wave.
- Enjoy damn good scones and butter.
- Read a racy novel.
- Have a game of chess.

He said, she said . . .

'There's a touch of the artist about old Bloom.'

A WANDERING DUBLINER

Titbit

This chapter has been compared to a game of chess. The Viceroy's carriage represents the wily king, the priest dashes about, and everybody else is a pawn.

May I say a word to your telephone, missy?

Sweets of Sin

Sirens
The one with music everywhere

Location 11: The Ormond Hotel on Ormond Quay

What's the story?

On his way to his rendezvous with Molly, Blazes Boylan pops into a hotel bar for a quick drink. Bloom secretly follows him in and stays for a steak and kidney pie. Stephen's dad and his friends enjoy a sing-song around the piano. The barmaids, Miss Lydia Douce and Miss Mina Kennedy, flirt with the punters while flashing a bit of leg and pulling suggestively on the beer pumps. Back out on the street, Bloom farts along to the sound of a tram.

Why don't you . . . ?

- Sing 'Love's Old Sweet Song' in a bar.
- Eat a steak and kidney pie and wash it down with a bottle of cider.
- Make music with a fart.

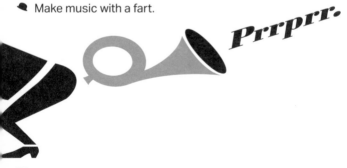

Prrprr.

He said, she said . . .

'Sure, you'd burst the tympanum of her ear, man . . . with an organ like yours.'

STEPHEN DEDALUS'S DAD

Titbit

Joyce was a great singer, winning a bronze medal at the Feis Ceoil in 1904. His wife Nora wished he had pursued singing instead of writing. The opening pages of this chapter sound like an orchestra tuning their instruments before a performance.

Cyclops
The one with the fight

Location 12: Barney Kiernan's pub on Little Britain Street

What's the story?

Bloom goes into the pub where the Citizen and his dog Garryowen are propped up against the bar. Afternoon pints and gossip flow freely. Bloom pretends to be oblivious to taunts from the barflies about his wife's affair and his supposed win on the horse Throwaway. The Citizen rants about nationalism and attacks Bloom for being Jewish. Bloom fights back with a verbal blow as he runs out of the pub, followed by Garryowen and a biscuit tin.

Why don't you . . . ?

- Go for an afternoon pint.
- Curse in Irish, *Póg mo thóin ríoga na hÉireann!* (Kiss my royal Irish arse)
- Strike up a conversation with the regulars.
- Visit the Jewish Museum on Walworth Road.

38

He said, she said . . .

'I was blue mouldy for the want of that pint. Declare to God I could hear it hit the pit of my stomach with a click.'

A BARFLY

Titbit

Joyce and Ernest Hemingway were drinking buddies in Paris. Rumour has it that at the first sign of trouble Joyce would jump behind him and shout, 'Deal with him, Hemingway. Deal with him!'

Where is he till I murder him?

Part 3

EVImagesNING

'The summer evening had begun
to fold the world in its mysterious embrace.
Far away in the west the sun was setting and
the last glow of all too fleeting day
lingered lovingly on sea and strand . . .'

Nausicaa
The one with the climax

8pm

Location 13: Sandymount Strand

What's the story?

Full of romantic dreams, young Gerty MacDowell lies on the beach with friends and their children. A religious ceremony is taking place in a nearby church as a bat flitters about in the dusk. Gerty's fantasies entwine with the eager eye and shifty hand of a dark, mysterious stranger. The prayers grow louder as fireworks climax overhead. Who's the man? Bloom. At it again! In his post-orgasmic stupor, he reflects on Molly's affair.

Why don't you . . . ?

- Build a sandcastle.
- Have improper thoughts in a public place.
- Check out the plaque at 22 Dromard Avenue in Sandymount, where Joyce spent the night on 16 June 1904.

She imagined . . .

'He was eying her as a snake eyes its prey. Her woman's instinct told her that she had raised the devil in him . . .'

GERTY MACDOWELL

Titbit

Joyce wrote, 'I've put in so many enigmas and puzzles that it will keep the professors busy for centuries.' In this episode, a swooping bat, a mysterious man and a sexually aroused young woman hint at Bram Stoker's *Dracula*.

And then a rocket sprang and bang shot blind and O! then the Roman candle burst and it was like a sigh of O! and everyone cried O! O!

Oxen of the Sun
The one with all the booze

Location 14: Holles Street Hospital

What's the story?

Bloom visits a friend who is due to give birth, but gets roped into the rowdy shenanigans of a group of medical students that include Stephen and Buck Mulligan. A nurse tells them to keep it quiet. As Stephen gets wasted, Bloom's paternal instincts are aroused. The men head for the pub for more 'bluggy drunkables' as language swills in the bottom of a pint glass.

Why don't you . . . ?

- Find Joyce's birthplace at 41 Brighton Square in Rathgar and Bloom's fictitious birthplace at Upper Clanbrassil Street.
- Speak in ye olde English.
- Get creative and give birth to something new.
- Enjoy a mix of drinks.

He said, she said . . .

'Come on, you winefizzling ginsizzling booseguzzling existences!'

STEPHEN DEDALUS

Titbit

This episode is a stampede through the English language from Anglo-Saxon to American slang. Joyce squeezed every literary technique and style into *Ulysses*. He made up his own words and drove the editors of the *Oxford English Dictionary* mad.

Bless me, I'm all of a wibbly wobbly.

Part 4

'We walk through ourselves, meeting robbers, ghosts, giants,
old men, young men, wives, widows, brothers-in-love.
But always meeting ourselves.'

Circe
The one in the brothel

Location 15: Monto

What's the story?

Bloom follows Stephen on a surreal waltz through Nighttown, where characters change costume and gender before his eyes. Midsummer madness! Bloom is put on trial. Decomposing Paddy Dignam comes to his defence. Found guilty, Bloom is declared pregnant and crowned King of Ireland. He finds Stephen in a brothel where Bella Cohen, the madam, dominates Bloom. Stephen fights the ghost of his mother and a British soldier. Having faced their demons, our two heroes leave Monto together.

Why don't you . . . ?

- Dance with someone.
- Check out Milo O'Shea's handprints outside the Gaiety Theatre on South King Street. He played Bloom in the 1967 film version of *Ulysses*.
- Dress up in drag.

He said, she said . . .

'Has little mousey any tickles tonight?'
A YOUNG PROSTITUTE

Titbit

In 1904, Monto was Europe's largest red-light district. In *Ulysses*, Joyce called it 'Nighttown', which was slang among Dublin journalists for the night shift on a newspaper.

Eumaeus
The one with the seaman

Location 16: A cabmen's shelter near Butt Bridge

What's the story?

Bloom and Stephen are knackered after a long day – Bloom ridiculously sober, Stephen completely drunk. They get the late-night munchies and have dodgy coffee and stale buns in a cabmen's shelter. Their conversation goes nowhere as boredom oozes out of the floorboards. WB Murphy, a tough old sailor, weaves tall tales as he shows off his tattoos and pisses loudly in the gutter. As Bloom and Stephen head out into the night, a horse takes a big shit.

Ate by sharks after.

He's gone too.

I seen a crocodile bite the fluke of an anchor . . .

Why don't you . . . ?

- Drink cold coffee and eat dodgy buns.

- Take turns to tell tall tales.

- Show off your tattoos.

He said, she said . . .

'Every country, they say, our own distressful included, has the government it deserves.'

LEOPOLD BLOOM

Titbit

In 1875, cabmen's shelters were built to prevent the drivers of carriages for hire from meeting in the local pub during bad weather. They served hot food and non-alcoholic drinks to keep the cabbies from drinking on the job. Some of the shelters can still be spotted around London.

Ithaca
The one under the stars

Location 17: 7 Eccles Street

What's the story?

Bloom takes Stephen home and puts on the kettle. They talk. They don't talk. They drink cocoa. They take a piss under the stars. Bloom offers Stephen the couch. He declines and disappears into the night. Bloom potters around the kitchen reflecting on the day. He climbs into bed with Molly, wiping another man's crumbs from the sheets. He kisses her bum. He is home. Drifts off . . . to . . . sleep.

Why don't you . . . ?

- Discuss life over a mug of cocoa.
- Gaze at the stars while taking a piss.
- Kiss somebody on the cheek.
- Sleep top to tail.

He thought . . .

'Womb? Weary? He rests. He has travelled.'
LEOPOLD BLOOM

Titbit

Joyce often wrote sprawled across the bed with domestic chaos all around him. Nora moaned that he kept her awake all night, chuckling to himself while composing *Ulysses*.

The heaventree of stars
hung with humid
nightblue fruit.

Penelope
The one with herself

Location 18: 7 Eccles Street

What's the story?

Awake in the middle of the night, Molly's mind and hands wander about. She thinks about Blazes Boylan and his big red brute of a thing. She fantasises about doing it with a priest. She farts. She dreams up filthy words she would use to spice up her sex life. She and Bloom haven't done it since their baby son died. Her thoughts turn to Bloom's lovable quirks, and she recalls the day he proposed to her on Howth Head. She said YES.

Why don't you . . . ?

- Visit Galway, the home town of Nora Barnacle.
- Spot the ghost sign for Finn's Hotel on South Leinster Street, where Nora Barnacle was working when she met Joyce.
- Take a day trip to Howth Head.
- Say YES!

She thought . . .

'Theres nothing like a kiss long and hot down to your soul . . .'
MOLLY BLOOM

James Joyce arranged to meet Nora Barnacle on the steps of Oscar Wilde's family home on Merrion Square for a first date. She stood him up, but inspired Joyce to write *Ulysses*, a celebration of Dublin life on 16 June 1904, the day she finally turned up.

And yes
I said yes
I will
Yes.

'Life, love, voyage round your own little world.'
LEOPOLD BLOOM

'Most beautiful book come out of Ireland my time.'
BUCK MULLIGAN

'It is a revolting record of a disgusting phase of civilisation;
but it is a truthful one.'
GEORGE BERNARD SHAW

'It is a positively brilliant and hellish monster-birth.'
CARL JUNG

'Racier than one of mine.'
PAUL DE KOCK

About At it Again!

We are Irish-German creative couple Niall Laverty and Maite López. We write, illustrate and self-publish our literary guides and gifts in Dublin, Ireland. Niall likes to twirl his moustache as he dreams up visual puns, and Maite eats books for breakfast washed down with a mug of coffee.

We want to give you a peek through the keyhole into the world of Irish literature to inspire you to discover and explore Irish authors, their books and the places that influenced them. We bring a fresh twist and a pinch of naughtiness to Irish literature by distilling its essence through our unique mix of writing, illustration and design with our pocket guides and literary gifts.

All our literary guides and gifts are created and printed in Ireland using vegetable-oil-based inks on carbon-neutral, acid-free, 100% recycled and FSC-certified paper.

Thanks to

Niels Caul, Amy Fox, Liz Hudson, Ronan McDonnell and Ciarán Smith.

NOTES

NOTES